Today I Will Moo

visit us at **www.flyingrhino.com**

Copyright ©2000 Flying Rhinoceros, Inc.

All rights reserved. Farmer Bob and Flying Rhinoceros are trademarks of Flying Rhinoceros, Inc.

Mailing Address: P.O. Box 3989
Portland, Oregon
97208-3989

E-mail Address: bigfan@flyingrhino.com

Library of Congress Control Number: 98-094847

ISBN 1-883772-19-2

Printed in Mexico

2

Farmer Bob has a friend named Jenny.
Jenny the Dog helps Farmer Bob run his farm.

Big Purple Barns

Barns are used for many things. Animals live in barns. Hay and grain are stored in barns. Farm tools are stored in barns. Barns are painted to protect them from the weather. Many barns are red. They can also be painted white, blue, yellow, or even purple!

4

One day, while helping Farmer Bob,
Jenny saw something strange.
Sam the Ram stood on a big bale of hay.
Sam cleared his throat and said,
"I am tired of making the same sound every day."

"Today I will moo!"

Stalls
A stall is a small room inside a barn.
Farm animals can eat or sleep in a stall.

Home Sweet Home
Animals on a farm have a
place to live:

Chicken ⟶ Coop
Horse ⟶ Stable
Sheep ⟶ Fold
Pig ⟶ Pen
Rabbit ⟶ Hutch

A Dog's Best Friend
Dogs can have many jobs on a farm.
A dog can also be a farmer's friend.

Guard Duty
On some farms dogs help
to protect animals.

6

Sam began to moo. He was very loud.
This made Jenny nervous. She thought the other
animals would be confused if they heard
Sam the Ram say, "Moo!"

A Hard Day Herding
Some dogs help farmers herd
flocks of sheep.

Pest Patrol
Mice and rats eat crops and animal feed.
Cats live on the farm and keep rats and
mice away from feed and crops.

7

A sheep's coat of wool is called a fleece.

Family Facts
Male sheep: Ram
Female sheep: Ewe
Baby sheep: Lamb

Flock
A group of sheep
is called a flock.

Thanks for Shearing!
When it is time to get the wool from
sheep, the sheep are given haircuts.
This is called shearing.

Sam kept on mooing. He mooed very loudly.
Soon his strange mooing attracted a crowd.
The other animals came to hear Sam.
A mooing sheep was something new.

This was not right. If the ram changed his sound, then maybe the other animals should make new sounds too.

Horses only breathe through their noses.

Big Toe

Horses, donkeys, and mules have only one toe on each foot. The toe is covered by a big toenail, called a hoof. Hooves need to be trimmed just like our toenails.

Family Facts

Male horse: Stallion
Female horse: Mare
Baby horse: Foal

"If Sam says "Moo," then what should I do?"
asked Carmen the Cow.
"I can not make a sound that a sheep is making."
Carmen decided to choose a new sound to make.

Horsing Around
Horses can pull plows and
farm machinery. Some people
like to ride horses for fun.

Hands Above the Rest
Horses are measured in units called
hands. One hand is four inches.

"Oink" said Carmen. "Oink! Oink! Oink!"
"If Sam can be a cow, then I will be a pig."
Carmen rolled around in some mud.
She ate slop from a pail.
She tried very hard to put a curl in her tail.

Guts, Guts, Guts!
Cows have stomachs with four parts: the rumen, reticulum, omasum, and abomasum.

I Think I'll Have Seconds
Cows chew their food twice. After they chew and swallow it the first time, it comes back up and they chew it again. The chewed food is called cud. A cow spends up to 8 hours a day chewing its cud.

Family Facts
Male cow: Bull
Female cow: Cow
Baby cow: Calf

Foods That Come from Milk:
Butter
Cheese
Cream
Yogurt
Ice cream
Cottage cheese
Sour cream

A Real Pig
Cows spend up to 8 hours a day eating.

In Udder News
Cows make milk. The milk is stored in the cow's udder.

13

Then the pigs became confused. If Carmen the Cow was going to oink, what should they say? The pigs decided that it would be fun to be chickens. "Cluck, cluck, cluck!" said the pigs.

Family Facts
Male pig: Boar
Female pig: Sow
Baby pig: Piglet

Sweating Like a Pig
Pigs don't sweat like people. They can only sweat through their noses.

A Tail to Tell
To tell how a pig is feeling, look at its tail!
Happy or excited ⟶ Curly
Sad or mad ⟶ Straight and stiff
Content ⟶ Hanging down, even wagging

The pigs packed up their bags
and moved into the chicken coop.

Smarter than smart
Pigs are very smart. Some people
keep pigs as pets.

Dirty Little Pig
Pigs are really clean animals. They
only roll in the mud to keep cool.

The pigs ran around the chicken coop, saying,
"Cluck, cluck, cluck!" and "Cock-a-doodle-doo!"
"If the pigs are clucking, what should we do?" asked
the chickens. One of the chickens began to bark.
Soon the other chickens began to bark, sniff, and growl.
Then all of the chickens moved into Jenny's doghouse.

"Eggsellent"
Only hens lay eggs. Eggs come
in many colors. Different kinds
of hens lay different colors of
eggs. Eggs can be white, brown,
blue, or even green.

16

Alarm Clock
Roosters crow when the sun comes up.
They also crow to warn or dare other
animals. Sometimes they crow just for fun!

Mother Hen
A hen sits on her eggs to keep them warm so they will hatch. This is called setting.

Family Facts
Male chicken: Rooster
Female chicken: Hen
Baby chicken: Chick

17

The farm was a mess.
Jenny the Dog was very upset.
The animals were all making strange noises.
Worst of all, Jenny's house was full of chickens!

"I can't make the animals
make their own noises," said Jenny.
"Dr. Patchit, the vet, can't make
the animals make their own noises.
I don't know what I should do.
This farm is a mess—all thanks to Sam,
the ram who says moo!"

19

"The chicks all bark.
The ducks say meow.
We even have a cow who oinks!
Nobody here is doing their job.
The person I need is my friend, Farmer Bob."

oink oink oink oink oink oink oink oink oink oink

Hisssss!

BARK!

BARK!

BARK!

BARK!

BARK!

Jenny ran to find Farmer Bob. She told him about the big mess back at the farm. Farmer Bob drove home on his tractor as fast as he could.

Long Ago...
People and animals used to do all the work on the farm. Now farmers use machines to do lots of jobs.

A Real Workhorse
Farmers use tractors to pull other machines, such as plows and seed drills.

22

Jenny gathered all of the animals in the barnyard.
Farmer Bob told all of the animals that it was
all right to try new sounds.

Big Weeder
A cultivator is used to dig up weeds and loosen soil. This helps plants while they are growing.

Know the Drill
A seed drill helps plant seeds into neat rows.

Can You Dig it?
A plow is used to dig up soil. This helps mix air and water into the soil.

"It is fun to try different and exciting things.
But it is also important that we all do our jobs.
I need pigs to say oink.
My chickens should lay eggs.
The cows need to make milk.
The sheep should grow wool."

Cropping Up
Farmers gather their ripe crops. This is called harvesting.

Eat your Leaves
Vegetables are the parts of the plant you eat. We eat leaves, stems, stalks, and roots of plants.

Grow Up
Plants need air, water, soil, and sunshine to grow.

24

Fields of Food

Crops are plants that farmers grow. Some crops are corn, apples, carrots, and Brussels sprouts. Farmers grow all kinds of crops so that we have many different foods to eat.

"Jenny needs to help me run the farm,
and none of us would know when to get up
in the morning without a cock-a-doodle-doo!"

"You are all very special.
Do what you do best."

27

Things settled down after Farmer Bob's speech.
The animals all went back
to their own jobs and sounds.

This had been a crazy day.
Jenny was very tired. Her job was now done,
so she decided to take a nap. She curled up under
a big shade tree. She was just about ready
to fall asleep when she heard a strange noise...

ABOUT THE AUTHORS AND ARTISTS

 Ben Adams says farm animals are smelly, but he likes to draw pictures of them anyway. Ben lives in his very own house in Portland, Oregon. He likes to spend time in his backyard pruning, watering, and sculpting his trees into giant farm animals. Someday, he hopes to have his own tree farm and change his name to Farmer Ben.

 Julie Hansen grew up in Tillamook, Oregon, and knows a lot about cows. Although she has never actually owned a cow, she has raised almost everything else: dogs, cats, chickens, rabbits, frogs, rats, mice, fish, ducks, snakes, squirrels, and the occasional muskrat. She lives in Salem, Oregon with her husband, Mark, their son, Chance, two cats, and a dog the size of a cat.

 Kyle Holveck lives in Newberg, Oregon, with his wife, Raydene, and their daughter, Kylie. In Newberg, there are lots of farms and animals. Kyle's favorite farm animal is the rhinoceros, which *we* know is not really a farm animal. Because his house is too small to keep a rhinoceros, Kyle has a chihuahua named Pedro instead.

 Aaron Peeples's hero is Farmer Bob. He says that any man who can look good wearing overalls day after day is definitely a great man. Aaron is currently attending college in Portland, Oregon, and he enjoys drawing farm animals at Flying Rhinoceros between classes.

 Ray Nelson thinks cows and pigs are really neat. He also thinks bacon and hamburgers are really neat. (We haven't told him where bacon and hamburgers come from yet.) Ray lives in Wilsonville, Oregon, with his wife, Theresa. They have two children, Alexandria and Zach, and a mutant dog named Molly.

CONTRIBUTORS: Melody Burchyski, Jennii Childs, Paul Diener, Lynnea "Mad Dog" Eagle, MaryBeth Habecker, Mark Hansen, Lee Lagle, Mari McBurney, Mike McLane, Chris Nelson, Hillery Nye, Kari Rasmussen, Steve Sund, and Ranjy Thomas

visit us online:
www.flyingrhino.com
or call 1-800-537-4466